ERIN WINTERS
SOMETIMES I WANT A HUG

Illustrations and cover design by Kaitin Röckle

Paperback ISBN: 978-1-958702-39-0

SNOWFALL
PUBLICATIONS LLC

To deployed service members
and their families -
from one military family to another.

I thought I'd be strong, with a stiff upper lip,
when you left for your very long, far away trip.

I tried to be brave, but instead I was sad,
and I'm pretty sure sometimes I even was mad.

An unwelcome rumble was down in my tummy;

I suddenly felt just a little bit crummy.

It's confusing, this talk of farewells and goodbyes.

I'm not sure what they mean when they say that time flies.

I know it's okay to have feelings inside,
and sometimes I just want to run off and hide.

When that happens I know I have three special places -
Mom helped write them down, they are safe thinking spaces.

Emotions can feel really big, really strong,
so we thought up some ways we could help them along.

If we try not to feel them, they always come back,
but the trick is to guide them to go the right track.

When I feel out of sorts, here are things that I do:
first, I look for five things I can see in my view.

Next, I look for four things I can touch with my hand,
Then three things I can hear, like a voice or a fan.

On hard days I might squeeze my pillow real tight,
and you can squeeze yours when you miss me at night.

It is okay to miss you, to wish you were here,
and when you come home, we will shout and we'll cheer!

You left to protect us at work far away,
to keep us all safe, to keep danger away.

I know that you're busy, off helping us all,
but sometimes I want a hug more than a call.

Well, we've worked really hard
here on our side as well...
I've grown really tall -
as I'm sure you can tell!

I love making pictures and writing you letters,
and we even made our own holiday sweaters!

I cry and Mom gives extra hugs when I'm low,
then I pedal my bike just as fast as it goes!

I take breaths and I count and I cuddle our kitten,
and I love when the mail brings us letters you've written!

I picked out a gift just precisely for you,
and we packed it up safe with some bubble-wrap too!

It looks like the ornaments came from a store,
I made them myself (if you want, I'll make more)!

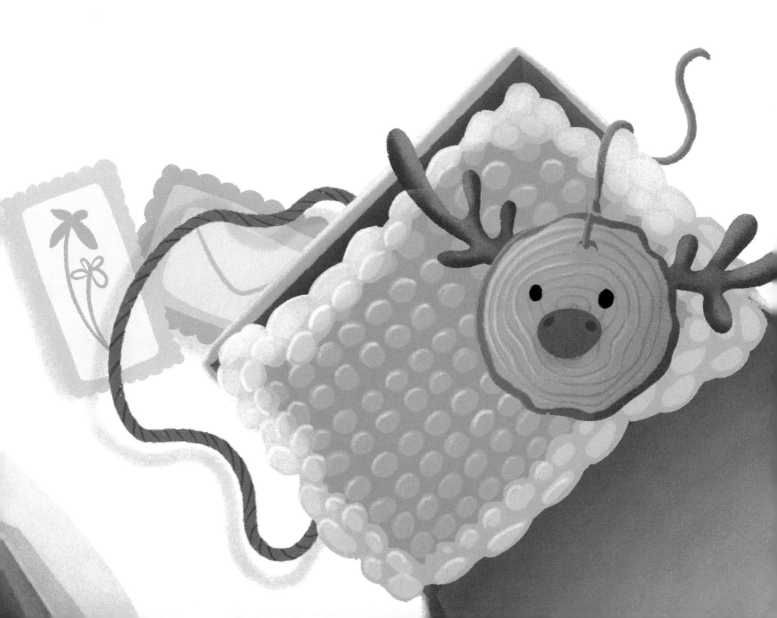

We get to eat one piece of candy each day
and Mom says when they're gone you'll be back home to play

I am making a list of the things we will do
when you're home again,
after your long trip is through!

Goodbyes are real hard, but I'm figuring out
that the going is not all this trip is about.

The **harder** it feels when you have to let go,
the more it will make for a **sweeter** hello.

Brainstorming Your Deployment

Deployments are hard. But if we work together, we can come up with things that help keep us connected and make us feel better on hard days!

- Video calls
- Voice recordings (if on a ship without WiFi, be sure to record more before departure)
- Countdown jar: every day, take a piece of candy from the jar, and when they're gone, deployment is over!
- Cross off days on a calendar
- Time zone clocks and maps on the wall for where the service member is and what time it is there
    - Deployment tree: use poster board to make a tree trunk, and fill the leaves with funny stories, memories, or things you want to do with the service member when they come home. Add to the tree over deployment, and at homecoming, you'll have a big list to share!
    - Recordings of the service member reading books for the kids
    - Mommy / Daddy Blanket: a blanket with photos of the service member and the child for the child to keep and snuggle

Which of these ideas is your favorite?
Circle the ones that sound the best!

- Write letters and draw pictures
- Send a care package
- Daddy dolls, frames, or stuffed animals special from the service member, especially with a voice recording inside
- Have the service member send letters or other packages/small gifts
- Send a stuffed animal with the service member for them to take pictures with and take on adventures
- Video messaging apps. These are particularly good because the family can send messages when convenient, showing what they're doing, and the service member can look when they have the chance, and respond, making the scheduling problems of time change easier. Kids can also scroll back and re-watch their favorite videos of their service member talking to them!
- Wall of hearts: every day, write something to the service member on construction paper hearts and hang it on the wall. When they come home, they'll be surprised by a wall full of sweet messages!
- Keep photos of the parent with the child accessible whenever they want to see them, whether framed, in a box, or printed on a "daddy doll" or photo blanket.

From Our Family To Yours

I wrote this book 3 days before my husband departed on our kids'
first deployment experience. The youngest had just turned 1,
and the oldest was 2.5.

What worked for us might not work for you, but it's important
to remember the time will pass, you'll find a new normal,
and you'll get back to your together-normal after homecoming.

Communicate as a couple and communicate as a family.
Talk about what to expect, and work through emotions as they arise
(yours and your child's).

We did it—and so can you!

Our Sweeter Hello

When homecoming starts to approach, it's a good idea to talk to your service member about what you are each hoping for.

Would they prefer the homecoming poster and welcome, or will they be dropped off on a bus at a smaller location with little fanfare? Do they want extended family there? Do you?

We all know that flexibility is the name of the game for all things military. Hold your plans loosely, but be on the same page as much as possible. And bring snacks and a couple toys to keep the kids occupied while you wait for the plane/bus/transportation to arrive!

FREE FEELINGS CHART

A tool for parents, caregivers, and clinicians.

Everyone has emotions! Sometimes it is hard to know what we are feeling and why. Learning about our emotions and talking about them with someone safe can help. This free resource is a great way to engage children in learning emotional regulation skills.

Erin Winters is a Licensed Professional Counselor, mom, and founder of Snowfall Publications LLC. Erin uses her clinical knowledge and experience to write high quality therapeutic children's books normalizing emotions and promoting mental health.

Erin has worked in a variety of mental health settingss including a child and adolescent psychiatric unit at a hospital, intensive in-home therapy, substance abuse programs for adults, and currently works in an outpatient setting with a variety of client ages, struggles, and goals.

When she isn't working or writing, Erin loves spending time with her husband and their two little boys, reading novels, and drinking hot chocolate.

OUR LATEST ADVENTURES

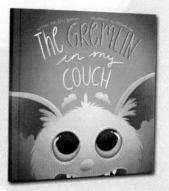

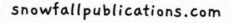

snowfallpublications.com

Made in the USA
Middletown, DE
28 March 2025